# CINDERELLA

Retold by Barbara Karlin

Illustrated by James Marshall

SCHOLASTIC INC.
New York  Toronto  London  Auckland  Sydney
Mexico City  New Delhi  Hong Kong

To Larry, Sean, and Joanna, for their enthusiasm,
and to Jim, without whom . . .

B.K.

ISBN 0-590-16255-1

Text copyright © 1989 by Barbara Karlin.
Illustrations copyright © 1989 by James Marshall.
All rights reserved.
Published by Scholastic Inc., 555 Broadway, New York, NY 10012, by
arrangement with Little, Brown and Company (Inc.).
SCHOLASTIC and associated logos are trademarks and/or registered
trademarks of Scholastic Inc.

15 14 13 12 11                    8 9 10/0

Printed in the U.S.A.

40

Once there was a widower
with a kind and beautiful daughter.
Life was sweet in their simple cottage,
until the widower decided to remarry.

Not knowing the ways of the world,
he married a vain and horrid woman,
whose two daughters were as vain and horrid as she.
"What a stupid little house!" they said.

The widower's daughter was made to work
like a servant in her own house.
She was soon run ragged — washing, ironing,
scrubbing, dusting, and cooking heaps of food.

The poor girl no longer had a bed of her own
and had to sleep among the ashes and cinders.
And from that time on,
they called her Cinderella.

Now it happened
that the king of the land
had a handsome son.
The king's greatest desire
was to see his son married.
He decided to give a ball
and invite all the fair maidens
of the realm.

When the king's messenger
delivered the royal invitation,
the dreadful stepsisters were overjoyed.
Each was convinced that
*she* would win the prince's favor.
On the day of the ball,
Cinderella was exhausted from trying
to make her stepsisters look beautiful.
"Wouldn't *you* like to go to the ball?"
they said, teasing her cruelly.
"Oh, yes!" said Cinderella.
"Don't be ridiculous!" cried the stepsisters.
"What would a wretched mouse like you
do at a fancy ball?"
And they shrieked with laughter.

Thinking themselves beautiful beyond words,
the stepsisters left for the ball.
"Don't be a lazybones while we're away,"
they said to Cinderella.
"And think about all the fun we'll be having."
After her stepsisters had gone,
Cinderella went about her chores.
As she worked, she wept bitterly.
"You look so miserable, child,"
said a kind voice.

"Who are you?" said Cinderella.
"I," replied the plump little woman,
"am your fairy godmother.
Please tell me why you are crying."
"I want *so* much to go to the ball,"
said Cinderella.
"That should not be too difficult to arrange,"
said the fairy godmother.
"But you must do as I say.
First, fetch me a nice, big pumpkin
from the garden."

Cinderella brought the biggest pumpkin
she could find.
"Now," said the fairy godmother,
"I will require six white mice
and a fine, fat rat."
Cinderella brought them,
live from the trap.
"And finally,"
said the fairy godmother,
"I must have two lizards.
You might look behind the watering pail."
Cinderella did as she was told.

With a touch of her wand,
the fairy godmother changed the pumpkin
into a magnificent golden coach,
the mice into six white horses,
the rat into a jolly coachman,
and the lizards into two sleek footmen.
"Lovely," the fairy godmother exclaimed. "Off you go!"
"Am I to go in rags?" said Cinderella.
"Silly me," said the fairy godmother.
And she transformed Cinderella's filthy rags
into an elegant gown and on her feet
placed a pair of sparkling glass slippers.
"*Now* you are ready," said the fairy godmother.
"But remember this — you must return home
before the stroke of midnight,
for then all your finery will change back to what it was."
Cinderella promised to obey
and then she was off to the ball.

At the palace, the prince learned
that an enchanting maiden had arrived,
and he greeted her himself.
The other guests were puzzled.
Who was this beautiful stranger?

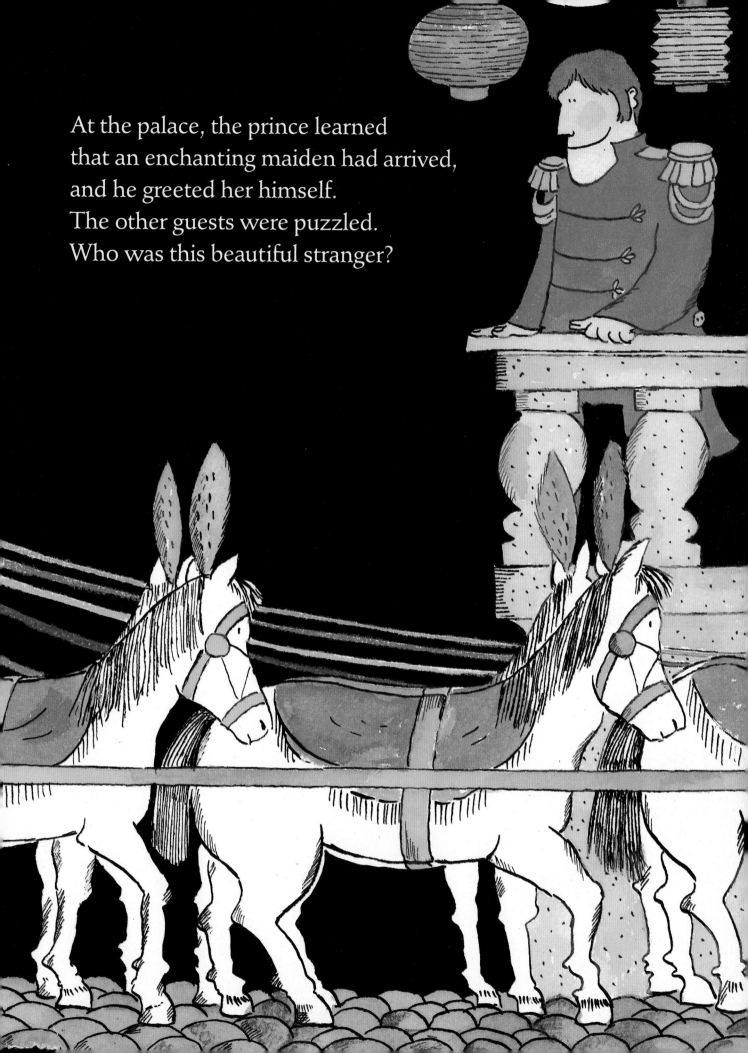

Completely smitten, the prince had eyes
only for Cinderella.
They danced every dance.
Cinderella found herself deeply in love.
She was so happy that she took no notice
of the hour.
Suddenly the clock began to strike twelve!

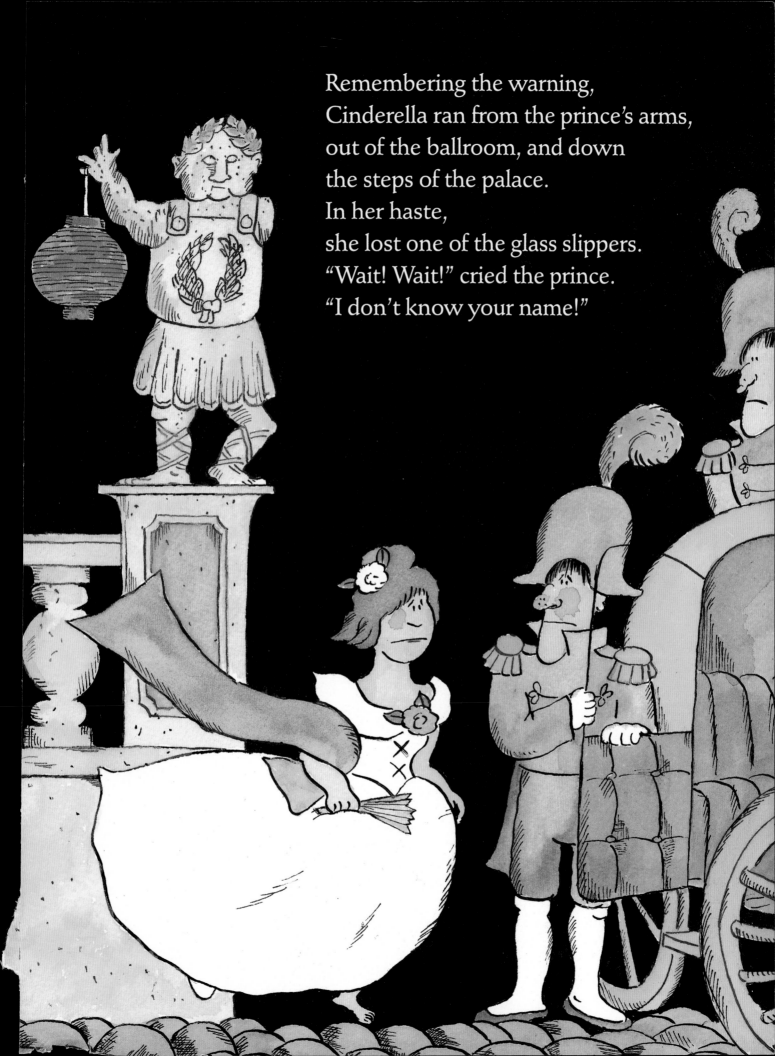

Remembering the warning,
Cinderella ran from the prince's arms,
out of the ballroom, and down
the steps of the palace.
In her haste,
she lost one of the glass slippers.
"Wait! Wait!" cried the prince.
"I don't know your name!"

Cinderella's golden coach sped away
from the palace.
But at the stroke of twelve
the fairy godmother's warning came true —
the coach was changed back into a pumpkin,
the horses back into mice,
the coachman back into a rat,
and the footmen back into lizards.
Cinderella was once again dressed in rags.

Discovering the tiny glass slipper, the prince vowed
to find and marry the beautiful stranger.
He traveled the kingdom far and wide,
trying the slipper on every maiden's foot.
But it fit no one.
Finally he arrived at Cinderella's house.
"Me first!" cried the elder stepsister,
extending her long, skinny foot.
But she could manage to get only
her toes into the slipper.
"My turn!" cried the younger stepsister,
thrusting her pudgy foot at the prince.
She pushed and shoved, grunted and groaned,
but the slipper would not fit.
"May I try it on?" said Cinderella,
stepping out of the shadows.

The glass slipper fit perfectly
on Cinderella's tiny foot.
"I have found my princess!"
cried the prince.
"We shall wed tomorrow!"
On that festive day, the kingdom rejoiced.
Generous and forgiving, Cinderella moved her family
into the palace and found a lord of the court
for each of her stepsisters to marry.

Cinderella's fairy godmother moved in too,
just to make sure everyone lived happily ever after.